BENJAMIN & TULIP

Dial Books for Young Readers
New York

BENJAMIN
& TULIP

by ROSEMARY WELLS

Every time Benjamin passed
Tulip's house, she said,
"I'm gonna beat you up."

And she did.

"Looks like he's been in a fight with Tulip again,
  and it looks like he got the worst of it,"
  said sister Natalie.
"That sweet little girl," said Aunt Fern.

Benjamin was cleaned up and sent to the store.

But first he had to go
past Tulip's house.
"This is my brand-new suit,"
said Benjamin.

"I'm gonna mess it up!" said Tulip.

And she did.

Benjamin went on to the grocery store in a daze.

"One watermelon, please," said Benjamin.
"How about some soap?" asked the grocer.

On the way back Benjamin
had to pass Tulip's house.
He held the watermelon over his head.
Maybe she won't know who I am,
he thought.

But she did.

"Where is the watermelon?" asked Aunt Fern.
"Back a ways," said Benjamin.

"This time," said Aunt Fern, "come back *with* the watermelon and *without* bothering that sweet little Tulip, or you can forget about dinner tonight."

Benjamin went back to fetch his melon.
When he saw Tulip, he zipped up
the nearest tree.

"You're cruising for a bruising!" said Tulip.
"I've got all night," Benjamin sighed.
"I won't get dinner now anyway."

"I'm coming to get you!"
Tulip growled.

"Get out of that melon
    and let me up!" said Tulip.
"I can't hear you,"
    said Benjamin.

"I'll give you three to get out of
that melon!" Tulip shrieked.
"Wait till I get out of this melon,"
said Benjamin.

"There!"